Alice Furlong

Roses and Rue

Alice Furlong

Roses and Rue

ISBN/EAN: 9783337078652

Printed in Europe, USA, Canada, Australia, Japan

Cover: Foto ©Andreas Hilbeck / pixelio.de

More available books at **www.hansebooks.com**

ROSES AND RUE

BY

ALICE FURLONG

LONDON
ELKIN MATHEWS, VIGO STREET
1899

To My Dead Mother

She for whom my book is writ,
In her heaven golden-lit,
Sure will smile for thought of it.

Grief and gladness both were hers,
I have gathered up the tears
And the laughter of dead years.

If my rhyming holy is,
Then my mouth hath kept the bliss
Of my dear saint's dying kiss.

And if a strain from Paradise
Wanders through it or underlies,
She is speaking in this wise.

Contents

vii

The Trees

THESE be God's fair, high palaces,
　　Walled with fine leafy trellises,
Interstarred with the warm and luminous azure ;
Sunlights come laughing through,
And rains and honey-dew
Scatter pale pearls at every green embrasure.

The tangled twist and twine
Of His soaring staircases have mosses fine
For emerald pavement, and each leafy chamber
Is atmosphered with amber.
Athwart the iridescent air
The twinkling gossamer
Doth shimmer and shine
In many a jewelly line.

The chaffinch is God's little page.
O joyant vassalage !
" Your Will !　Your Will ! " he saith the whole
　　day long,
In sweet, monotonous song.
Poised on the window-sills of outmost leaves
He watches where the tremulous sunlight weaves

Its golden webbing over the palpitant grass,
While the Summer butterfly, winged of the
    blue-veined snow,
Like a fairy ship with its delicate sails ablow,
Floats by on aerial tides as clear as glass.

From the break of morn,
Herein the blackbird is God's courtier,
With gold tongue ever astir,
Piping and praising
On his beakéd horn.
To do his Seigneur duty,
In mellow fluency and dulcet phrasing,
In pæans of passing beauty ;
As a chanting priest,
Chanting his matins i' the wane o' the night,
While slow, great winds of vibrant light
Sweep up the lilied east.

The dumb beast is God's guest,
And every tired creature seeking rest ;
The sheep, grown weary browsing,
The cattle, drouthy with heat,
One after one, lagging on listless feet,
Seek the green shadow of God's pleasant housing ;
While the thousand wingéd things of bough and
    air
Do find God's palace fair.

The Betrayal

WHEN you were weary, roaming the wide
world over,
I gave my fickle heart to a new lover.
Now they tell me that you are lying dead ;
O mountains fall on me and hide my head !

When you lay burning in the throes of fever,
He vowed me love by the willow-margined river ;
Death smote you there—here was your trust
betrayed.
O darkness, cover me, I am afraid !

Yea, in the hour of your supremest trial
I laughed with him ! The shadow on the dial
Stayed not, aghast at my dread ignorance ;
Nor man nor angel looked at me askance.

.　　.　　.　　.　　.

Under the mountains there is peace abiding,
Darkness shall be pavilion for my hiding,
Tears shall blot out the sin of broken faith,
The lips that falsely kissed, shall kiss but Death.

The Seeking of Tir-Na'n-Oge

(The Maid).

I N the Land of Youth the spiders are weaving
their webs in the windless woods.
(Fine webs the spiders are weaving.)
All in the grey of the twilit morn the dews are
falling in fairy floods,
On the leafy bough the dove is grieving.

Come, come, my share of the world!
To the Land of Youth that is over the hill,
Where the spiders are weaving their webs
dew-pearled,
And the cushat coos while the morn is still.

(The Boy).

To the Land of Youth was the way but pleasant,
sooth, it were good to go.
(Sooth, it were good, was the way but pleasant.)
But north and south and east and west the dark-
winged winds do beat and blow,
Nor sun shall light us, nor star, nor crescent.

Stay in the dūn that is warm and wide,
Earth's Winter shall wane and pass.
Beltane-day shall come as a bride,
And gather daisies from the dewy grass.

4

In the Land of Youth the rose-red apples bloom
  on the apple boughs.
(White at the heart are the rose-red apples.)
Droopt and bent are the branches grey where
  the honeyed breezes drowse,
Dreamy shadow the green grass dapples.

  Come, come, my share of the world!
  Earth's Winter is wan and chill.
  The fruit is ripe there, the bud is curled,
  In the Land of Youth that is over the hill.

(*The Boy*).

To the Land of Youth the way is weary over
  the hill of Death.
(Wild is the way, and long, and weary.)
Phantom rain on thy bosom white, phantom
  wind to snatch at thy breath,
Night and mist for our faring eerie.

  Thy milken feet are tender and weak
  To climb the hill in the ghostly storm.
  Keep the rose on thy ruddy cheek,
  Stay in the dūn that is wide and warm.

.   .   .   .   .

But out on the snow she led him forth:
And the winds blew out of the east and the west.
And the wind of darkness drew from the north. . . .
No man knoweth how fared the quest.

God's Poem

THIS is God's poem speaking to our hearts,
  A day in Spring, a clear, soft-breathing day.
The skies are shining pearl, a lucent veil
Before the hidden sun ; the cool, deep grass
Seemeth to hold the light within itself,
And in the meadow breaketh rapturously
Into gold flame of cowslips, starry fleck
Of clustering daisies.   Underneath the trees
No shadow is, but only dimmer light
Than in the open ; and the gentle wind
Whispereth softly, lest perchance it break
The quiet dreams of the freshly-budded leaves.
Then in the hush some little, flitting bird
Singeth out clear upon his silver pipe,
Or wooing doves in shady chestnut trees
Murmur in quiet tones of restful love ;
And the dear wanderer's " Cuckoo ! Cuckoo ! "
Falls through the listening spaces of still air,
The undulating line of sombre hills
Is dark against the luminous, white sky ;
My heart hath nigh turned traitor to the blue,
For sake of this pale heaven, so wanly pure,

So purely white, so whitely beautiful.
O come with me, my love, my dearest love !
And let us stray adown the ways of Spring,
My heart is singing with the birds to-day.

The Dreamer

A WIND that dies on the meadows lush,
  Trembling stars in the breathless hush!—
The maiden's sleeping face doth bloom
A sad, white lily in the gloom.

Along the limpid horizon borne
The first gold breathing of the morn!—
A lovely dawn of dreams doth creep
Athwart the darkness of her sleep.

In the dim shadow of the eaves
A quiet stir of lifted leaves!—
As in the old, belovéd days,
She wandereth by happy ways.

With half-awakened twitterings,
The young birds preen their folded wings!—
She giveth a forget-me-not
To him who long ago forgot.

Athwart the meadowy, dewy-sweet,
A wind comes wandering on light feet!—
For her the wind is from the south,
His kiss is kind upon her mouth.

In the bird's house of emerald
The sun is weaving webs of gold!—
He *never* coldly went apart!
She *never* broke her passionate heart!

Pipeth clear from the orchard close
A thrush in the bowers of white and rose!—
She waketh praying: " God is good,
With visions for my solitude."

For full delight of birds and flowers
The long day spins its golden hours.—
She serves the household destinies ;
The dream is happy in her eyes.

A Caoine for Owen Roe

HEAVY the housings about his bed,
  Cold the clay that will hide his head.
The sun was red in the sky at noon,
The crescent moon was dim with dread.

Through the blind night the banshee cried,
The death-watch beat in the wall by his side,
The priest had untied his bonds of sin,
And every window was open wide.

Over and done are the warrior's wars,
There is martyr's balm for the martyr's scars;
Brake the prison-bars, and on soaring wing,
His soul went singing among the stars.

Sing, O Angels, 'twixt stars and space!
Weep, O Lady, your love's dead face.
To the keening-place come the women of grief,
Keening the Chief of Hy-Nial's race.

We bear his body by road and rath,
We bear his body by glen and path;
Thrice hath the magpie cursed in his flight,
Black is the blight on the aftermath.

Weird and wild is the wail of woman,
Humbled the head of the haughty Roman.
Dark the omen and dark the vision,
In deep derision outlaughs the foeman.

Chant the death-chant, O friars grey!
House the Chief in the holy clay!
Moon, hide away! Be blind, O Sun!
Christ and country are slain to-day!

At Nazareth

JESUS and His Mother Mary
    In the ways of Nazareth.
Lo! a little bird unwary
Falleth wounded unto death,
At the feet of Mother Mary
In the streets of Nazareth.

One of many children speaketh:
" See, my stone hath brought it down!"
How it fluttereth and seeketh,
Hiding in the Woman's gown!
And it's blood the white hem streaketh,
As it were with red stars strewn!

Mother Mary bendeth kindly,
Lifteth up the trembling thing
With the bright eyes staring blindly,
And the blood-drops on each wing.
Bright eyes close and dim resignedly,
Ceaseth all the fluttering.

Daylight hours have wrought their number,
Woven out their golden rule;
Shadow lieth, green and umber,
Round about the reedy pool;
"Infant Jesus, wake from slumber,
Sun hath set and eve is cool."

"Here, where grass is fresh and luscious,
Sit thee, whilst the pail I fill
From the dark pool by the rushes;
To thy breast hold very still
This most luckless of all thrushes
Village boys have used so ill."

Oh, His eyes are wide with wonder
At the cruelty of men!
Pale green rushes bend asunder,
Oh, His eyes are dark with pain!
Mary's pail goes dipping under,
Oh, His tears fall down like rain!

Dripping still from blood-soaked feather
To the dimpled baby-throat,
Sunlight and the snow together
Never were as white, I wot;
Nor the hawthorn in May weather
Blowing in the sheltered moat.

But the brown head hangeth meekly,
And the fluttered heart is numb;
And the brown wing droopeth sleekly,
And the mellow throat is dumb.
To the frail things and the weakly
Hurt and harm are sure to come.

Then the blessed Infant Jesus
Kisseth it with ruddy mouth;
Like the lush, dew-laden breezes
From the mountains of the south,
Soft His kiss; and oh, it pleases
As cool waters in the drouth!

At the heart doth death's dread weight weigh?
This Child's Hand may lift the load.
Lo! the bird is living straightway.
Two go down the darkening road,
Underneath the village gate-way,
Pondering on the things of God.

The Lonely One

A YEAR and a day she is in the burying-place,
　My heart is nigh breaking for a sight of
　　her face.
And sometimes I think—may God forgive the
　　sin !—
That in heaven they forget kith and kin.

They said : time is kind, this longing pitiful,
This agony of wishing will grow faint and dull.
They said : time is swift and the years fly like
　　birds.
Alas ! alas ! for men's idle words.

If the thorn be in the wound, how shall the
　　pain be dulled ?
In the midst of the dry wood, how shall the fire
　　be cooled ?
And can the birds fly swift if their wings droop
　　with pain,
And the night be wild with storm and thick
　　with rain ?

Perhaps they speak truth ; but my heart is just
　　as sore
As on the day they carried her coffin through
　　the door.

Perhaps they speak truth ; but the time is heavy
and slow,
In the Summer and the Autumn and the snow.

My darling, my darling, is the time long to you ?
Does your heart never weary beneath the grass
and dew ?
When the larks awake for morn and the light is
in the skies,
Are you willing to awaken and arise ?

The blackbird is building her nest in the hedge,
The little goslings swim at the grey water's edge.
The dun kine are pasturing along the headland's
brow,
And the rook is in the track of the plough.

Within your shady garden the rose, red and
sweet,
Hushes her heart to listen for the fall of your
feet,
Holding herself in waiting for the gathering of
your hand,
Poor rose, she does not understand !

Beside your dairy window the woodbines peeping
through,
Gather up their honey for their morning kiss
to you,
O honey-suckles, waiting for her at the window-
pane,
She will never, never, never come again !

Ireland in America

I'M a Judge in Boston city, I've a countless
    hoard of dollars;
I go northward in the Summer, I go southward
    in the snow.
I've the smartest fur-trimmed overcoats, the
    whitest linen collars,
I enjoy the best society with Presidents and
    scholars,
And the people shout "God bless him!" as I go.

The lawyers call me Solomon, the merchants
    call me Crœsus;
I'm "most affable" to journalists when I am
    interviewed;
I can never pass the fashionable, photo-selling
    places,
But I'm smilingly confronted by my daughters'
    pretty faces.
They're exhibited in every attitude.

There's a queenly, quiet lady who is hostess at
    my table,
Who is mistress of my household, who is
    mother of my girls,
(Gentle wife!) she dresses finer than the prin-
    cess in a fable,

Oh, the shimmer of her satin and the richness
of her sable !
Oh, the glory of her diamonds and her pearls !

I have all that man can wish for, I am honoured
and respected
By the highest and the lowest, by the freeman
and the slave,
They put me down Vice-President for each new
work projected,
For next session of the Congress I am sure to
be elected -
Oh, my lost green land, my land beyond the wave !

Perhaps my eyes are age-dimmed, but I think
the dawn was whiter
Over Connemara's mountains than behind that
eastern range,
In the grey grass the young lark sang, with no
human to affright her,
Yea, in Connemara's mountains even the song-
bird's heart was lighter—
But in the strange land everything is strange.

I remember Summer evenings, when my mother
milked the " dhrimmin."
When the sun-rays on her white cap fell like
rose-light on the snow,
How I thought the blue eyes like to Her's, the
blessed amongst women,
And the red mouth bent and kissed me as the
twilight gathered dim in
Cool recesses where the fraughans hide and grow.

Then we hurry through the gloaming lest the
    leprechaun belate us,
And the sheep-dog runs before us on quick-
    pattering, eager feet,
For the father and the master and the supper
    all await us,
And no diamonds ever glistened like the froth
    on the potatoes
In the three-legged skillet on the fire of peat.

Little silver flames go trembling through the
    blocks of glowing amber,
Reach the unlit outer edges, strain beyond am-
    bitiously,
Rise like baby tides of moonlight, creep and fly
    and spring and clamber,
Lo! the firelight falls and flashes in the dusky,
    brown-roofed chamber—
And the gossoon laughs upon his father's knee!

Then I hear my mother whisper, " Let us bless
    Him who has blessed us ! "
And outside the corn-crake murmurs in the
    depths of dewy grass,
In the dim blue sky the stars come out while we
    lie down and rest us—
I've been dreaming ! here I'm sitting by my fire
    of stiff asbestos,
And my footman enters in to light the gas !

The Year's Children

Spring.

SHE is mild, she is mild!
   Creeping up the chilly lanes
In the silver of the rains.
All her hair is April-wild,
But a hint of golden May
Hides in tresses blown astray.
For the love of this young child
Blooms the daffodil
And the primrose on the hill.

Summer.

She is warm, she is warm!
Dancing from the bloomy south,
With the red rose on her mouth—
With the lovely, tearful charm
Of the unconsuméd dew
In her eyes of burning blue.
She hath courtiers—a swarm
Of the yellow bees
To make honey in her trees.

Autumn.

He is fire, he is fire!
Leaping over the high hills,
Where the red lark soars and trills.
Burns the berry on the brier,
And the gold mist of the wheat
Flickers softly round his feet.
He shall sate thy heart's desire,
Dropping slumber deep
From his flowers of rosy sleep.

Winter.

He is white, he is white!
Sweeping down in spangled snows,
(With the diamond and the rose
Shimmering through veils of light.)
Filmy, trailing draperies
He doth hang upon the trees.
In the mystic, middle night
He doth flash the stars'
Silver-frosted scimitars.

Forsaken

THIS Autumn gloaming, the clouds grown weary of raining,
Sweep down behind the hill-tops, misty and blurred.
The wind has ceased its monotonous complaining,
Thrills through the twilight the sudden song of a bird.

Sudden and sweet fall the notes in a silver shower,
Dropping out on the silence—a marvellous rain!
Fairer than gleam of sunlight, than fragrance of flower,
Than whisper of waves on the strand, flows the beautiful strain.

My little bird, dost thou dream of the fair recesses
Of green, dim woodlands, where through the Summer day
The leaves sway tremulous in the wind's caresses,
Where through an emerald maze the sunbeams stray.

Dreamer, dost thou forget that the leaves are
  dying?
That sunbeams hide when skies are misty and
  sad?
That Winter cometh—dost hear the weird wind
  sighing
The Summer's death-song? Why is thy heart
  so glad?

I cannot sing with thee, robin: my heart is aching,
One who was here in Summer is not here now,
'Twas a sweet dream to me, ah, but a harsh
  awaking—
Sometimes I feel his hand upon my brow.

Just where he laid it once with touch so tender,
Looking into my eyes with bitter regret;
My heart went out to him with a swift surrender.
Ah, but he found it easy to forget!

Woe, for the love that cannot waver nor wander!
When snows are falling and Winter nights are
  here,
One shall sit by a lonely fireside and ponder
On the love that faded out with the fading year.

In a Lonely Land

WHO, weeping, sitteth desolate ?
Who, but the Irish mother
Keening her exiled children.
In her little, brown-thatched cabin,
Where the turf-smoke gathers in a mist,
A blue-grey, delicate mist, with a fragrant odour,
Shrouding in ghostly way the blackened rafters,
She sits and mourns,
Keening her departed ones :
Ullagone ! Ullagone !

In the Autumn,
When the cold wind from the bogland
Creeps through the open door and breathes on
    the peat-blocks,
Fanning them into warm ruby, and clear-glowing
    amber,
She thinks of a night in October,
When Mary, the youngest and dearest
Of three blue-eyed daughters,
Stood at the door with tossed tresses, and crim-
    son lips parted,
Holding her apron full of ripe nuts

From the hazel bush by the river;
Her sweetheart was laughing beside her. . . . .
She wakes—the lonely mother !
Ullagone !   Ullagone !
Mary went over the seas years ago.
Her sweetheart (God rest him !) lies in the
   churchyard.

There were two brave boys :
They went one Summer morning ;
A lark was singing up in the sky,
The meadows were russet-shaded on the surface,
And luminous underneath,
As if they were on fire with soft, emerald light.
The mother saw it all :
And saw her sons pass out through the doorway.
She caught them to her heart and kissed them,
With passionate kisses.
Then a ship sailed over the green seas,
And over the blue seas,
And over the green seas again.
Lo ! the emigrants had reached the land of
   Columbus !
A beautiful land,
Where the sun is warm,
And the wheat ripens quickly,
And the blight never comes.
Where the earth is not accurst
With the tread of the conquerors' feet.
A beautiful land !
But the exiles, yearning for their own green Erin,
Love it not. . . . .
Wirrastrue !   The evening is dark,

And the wind is very lonely
Crying wearily at the window.
The woman's heart is sick
With the pain of love.
Slowly the rain drips through the holes in the
    thatch.
Ah! there are no strong hands to mend it now.
Ullagone! Ullagone!
For the widowed and childless
Weeping in life's November!
Dead leaves falling
Are not more hopeless than they.
Dead leaves drifting in an icy wind
Are not more pitiable.
Dead leaves under the snow
Are far happier.

Oh, the heart of an Irish mother!
It is as true as God,
And as sorrowful as Christ!

The Awakening

O SPRING will waken the heart of me
    With the rapture of blown violets!
When the green bud quickens on every tree,
The Spring will waken the heart of me,
And dews of honey will rain on the lea,
Tangling the grasses in silver nets.
Yes, Spring will waken the heart of me
With the rapture of blown violets!

In Memory of My Father

(James Walter Furlong,

*Who died at Steeven's Hospital, Dublin,
9th June,* 1897.)

LYING awake while the hours of darkness creep,
So many tears I weep
For you, down-stricken in life's midmost breath,
Brought dying to an ancient, cloistral place
That hath grown grey with looking in the face
Immutable Death.

Such bitter thoughts I have
Of you, my father, in the dread death-fight
Through the soft passing of a grey June night,
While I, in selfish sleep,
Had never a tear to weep,
Nor never a prayer to save
Your fevered mind from futile wanderings
Amid irrevocably-past, familiar things,
When God had set apart
Your happy, pardoned heart
For restful housing in a quiet grave.

If I had only known!
And surely if I loved you as I ought
Some wind of ill had wrecked the rosy thought
Sailing the still sea of my morning dreams
Like drifting buds upon the summer streams.
Ah God! a heart of stone
Had felt the passionate throb of anguished love
When those white lips did move,
To ask with hard-drawn breath,
And voice grown husky with the coming death;
" Give me a pencil, I must do my work!
Is this the second race ? "
The shapely hands were busy for a space—
Silent and cold and murk,
The night no man may work in drew apace.

If I had only known!
A stranger held your hands that grey night
          through,
To us, your very own,
Who had laid down our lives for love of you,
'Twas given but to reach you when you lay
Insentient as the clay
That was so cruelly soon to cover you.
We could but break our hearts in pity over you.

Whenever I pray in orphanhood bereaven
To Him of Whom is all paternity,
" Our Father, who art in heaven,"
Cometh—oh, very sweetly !—unto me
The smile that throned itself on your dead brows.
I know that Two are listening in God's House.

On Patrick's Day

ON Patrick's day as I came from Mass,
    The rain was fresh in the damp, green
        grass ;
But the wind-torn clouds left a rift of blue,
And the glistening sunbeams flooded through.

The strong, soft wind shook the grey boughs
    swinging,
And the warm, gold light set the robins singing;
The rain-clouds dark swept away to the east,
As I came from Mass on Patrick's feast.

Where the drifted clouds were grey and white
Shone the rainbow's arch of gleaming light,
Purple and primrose, green and red,
It flamed and burned in the sky o'erhead.

Then to my God I spake me thus.
" Lord, hast thou set this sign for us,
That we for sweet Ireland's sake may hope
Never again will the cloud-gates ope—"

" Loosing the fiercely-falling flood,
The blinding rain of tears and blood,
That poured on us through the long, dark years,
Sick with anguish, and hopes, and fears."

" Lord, may we hope, for sweet Ireland's sake,
That her pain is past, and her long heart-ache."
This was my prayer as I came my way
Home from Mass on Patrick's Day.

The World's Winter

" THIS our enlightened age:" the proud words
    pass
Over the lying lips from hearts of brass.
Good God! that white face hidden under the
    grass!

Silent, beautiful mouth, all marble-pale,
Open and speak: before your piteous tale
Methinks I see the boasters shrink and quail.

Dreaming eyes, will ye wake from your welcome
    sleep?
Come from your grave, O murdered one, and reap
Your vengeance! Smite the wolves that slay
    the sheep!

In my lord's country-house rose-scented air
Floated through open casements: here and there
Cool fountains gleamed and glimmered, silver
    and fair.

You gasped your soul out in the poisonous heat
Of a close garret in a filthy street,
Far from the winds and waters, fragrant and
    sweet.

When you lay pallid-faced, your strength all
    spent,
Water we gave you for strong nourishment:
You drank and smiled, and dying, were content.

Many a princely board that day was spread,
Where the wines glistened, amber and ruby-red,
Yea! and the very dogs were glutted with bread!

Three days were gone since you had eaten food,
The others revelled in their plenitude—
Shut fast their doors lest beggars should intrude.

The night came up from out the shadowy sea,
Creeping over the sad earth noiselessly,
And in that night God's pity set you free.

.   .   .   .   .

" This our enlightened age."   Ah, surely no!
While Christ's Belovéd starve and suffer so,
In Winter-time the dawn is faint and slow.

" My Share of the World "

I AM jealous: I am true:
    Sick at heart for love of you,
O my share of the world!
I am cold, oh, cold as stone
To all men save you alone.

Seven times slower creeps the day
When your face is far away,
O my share of the world!
Seven times darker falls the night
When you gladden not my sight.

Measureless my joy and pride
Would you choose me for your bride,
O my share of the world!
For your face is my delight,
Morn and even, noon and night.

To the dance and to the wake
Still I go but for your sake,
O my share of the world!
Just to see your face awhile,
Meet your eyes and win your smile.

And the gay word on my lip
Never lets my secret slip
To my share of the world !
Light my feet trip over the green—
But my heart cries in the keen !

My poor mother sighs anew
When my looks go after you,
O my share of the world !
And my father's brow grows black
When you smile and turn your back.

I would part with wealth and ease,
I would go beyond the seas,
For my share of the world !
I would leave my hearth and home
If he only whispered " Come ! "

Houseless under sun and dew,
I would beg my bread with you,
O my share of the world !
Houseless in the snow and storm,
Your heart's love would keep me warm.

I would pray and I would crave
To be with you in the grave,
O my share of the world !
I would go through fire and flood,
I would give up all but God
For my share of the world !

Home-Coming

BEYOND the Shannon's waters, dark and
sweet,
A little town doth nestle at the feet
Of a green hill whereon a tree-crowned wood
Maketh a still, thrush-haunted solitude.

One changeful April day of sun and rain,
With weak, slow steps you crossed the wild,
brown plain,
The kindly hill your innocent child-eyes knew
Lifted its emerald head to welcome you.

Did it not seem a little time ago
Since you were playing 'mid the daisy-snow
On green Roscommon slopes, finding the while
The whole world's sweetness in your mother's
smile.

Perchance 'mid the wild grandeur of the west
You longed for the Green Land: the fierce unrest
Of exile preyed upon you ceaselessly,
Urging you over leagues of tossing sea.

Perchance you craved in the strange, glorious
    land
To feel upon your brow a mother's hand,
To hear a mother's keen above your head
In passionate wailing o'er her placid dead.

Poor heart, awearying in that distant place,
With death's cold lips against your shrinking
    face !
Surely it was not strange that you should come
Over grey wastes of sea to die at home.

You journeyed over many a white-ridged wave
To sleep your death-sleep in an Irish grave ;
And kissed your Irish mother's loving lips
Before your light went dark in death's eclipse.

Honey-sweet was the breath of the Irish Spring !
Balm of the golden cowslips, blossoming
In wind-blown grass, out-floated on the air ;
The hawthorn buds were opening everywhere.

In the grey hills the larks sang, dawn and dusk;
The gorse-bloom burned its way through the
    dingy husk ;
The first wild rose flushed faint upon the briar
For love of amber eves and dawns of fire.

The fair Spring wooed you vainly—seven days,
And you were lying in the churchyard ways,
Where wind-swayed beeches chant a requiem
For the dead sleeping at the feet of them.

To Spring

SWEET Spring! with shy, soft eyes of heavenly
blue !
The wild winds whispered : " She is coming
here ! "
And laughed aloud for joy ; grey skies grew
clear,
The little streams woke up to welcome you.
The wan, gold primroses, all wet with dew,
Along the mossy margin of the mere
Crowded in fragrant clusters, and anear,
A tangle of white bloom, the wild-fire grew.

Now you have come. I hear by murmuring
streams
Your musical, low laugh, as silvery sweet
As the lark's singing in his rapturous dreams.
Where violets are thickest, there your feet
Have latest passed. The hare-bell's blue surprise
Echoes the laughter of your azure eyes.

Death and the Girl

The Girl.

I AM young to die; it is hard to go from the
singing of the thrush in the valleys,
I am young to die; it is hard to turn from the
rose that leans at the lattice.
The grave is dark and heavy the clay.
O the green world in the blooming May!

Death.

When the mist from the mountain the valley o'er-
shadeth, the thrush falleth silent for sorrow.
The rose at the lattice is lovely to-day, the rose
shall lie withered to-morrow.
Gladness shall slumber and grief shall waken,
Better forsake than be forsaken!

The Girl.

I am young to die; my mother's kiss is soft as
the wind on the meadow,
Her nearness is warmth to my frozen heart in
thy dread and sombre shadow.
Let me live: I would gather a rose that is good,
Love's rose on the tree of womanhood.

Death.

Live! And God give thee a heart of stone : for
    love than death is more bitter.
Thy wine shall be gall, and as ashes thy bread,
    and the sea than thy tears shall be sweeter.
Thou wilt gather for joyance, O girl forlorn,
A cankered rose with a spear-sharp thorn !

Yuletide

IN a stable bare,
   Lo, the great Ones are.
Strew the Ivy and the myrtle
Round about the Virgin's kirtle!

Ass and oxen mild
Breathe soft upon the Child!
Blow the scent of bygone summer
On your breath to the New-comer!

Be ye well content
To be straitly pent
Backwards in the rocky chamber
From the angel's wings of amber!

Rapt the seraphs sit,
With godly faces lit
In a radiance shining solely
From the Christ-child, meek and holy.

High they chant and clear
Of the lovely cheer
Ringing down the new evangels
Of the mystic, midnight angels.

Faring with good will
From the misty hill,
Every shepherd sacrificeth
To the prophet that ariseth.

Joseph, Mary's spouse,
Prince of David's House,
Bendeth low in adorations
To the Ruler of the Nations.

Who doth sweetly rest
On his Mother's breast,
Lord of the lightnings and the thunders!
Mary's heart keeps all these wonders.

All Souls' Night

IN a grave-yard lone
   Waileth a young maid;
With heart-piercing moan
Calling on her dead.

" Morn, noon, and even,
Heavy my hours creep.
In your happy Heaven,
Do you know I weep ? "

" All Souls' night is here,
Every spirit is free.
Leave God's House of cheer,
Travel home to me ! "

" Pass by every star
Shining like a seraph,
Moons that whitest are
Shun the tempting thereof."

" Be your journey swift.
I am waiting, blind.
You, my light, shall lift
The dark from my mind."

" Hush ! the midnight bell
The last chime hath given.
Yawneth deepest hell,
Opeth highest heaven."

" Some far sigh doth heave
Through the murky gloom.
Every ghost doth leave
Every mouldering tomb—"

" Greyly flits and goes
Like a wandering mist,
When the west wind blows
As its will doth list."

" O I fear these things !
And mine ears do hark
Rustle of phantom wings
Passing by on the dark ! "

" But come you . . . even as these.
Heart of me, my own !
Ah, my poor lips freeze
Kissing your grave-stone ! "

Cock-crow and red dawn.
The maid's dead face is grey.
All Souls' night is gone,
All saints smile to-day.

The Bard to his Beloved

LOVE of you and hate of you
  Tears my very heart in two !
As you please me or displease,
So I burn and so I freeze.

I would build your wattled dun
With a gold roof like the sun ;
I would stain the trellis bars
With the silver of the stars.

At my bitter heart's behoof
I would wreck your radiant roof ;
Of your twinkling trellises
All my anger jealous is.

I would give you great-horned rams,
Mild-eyed sheep, and milk-white lambs,
Fit for any king to own,
By the turning of the stone.

I would set your rams astray,
I would wile your sheep away,
With their lambs milk-white exceeding,
For the grey wolf's famished feeding.

45

I would guide the oxen meek,
And the ploughshares silver beak
O'er your land to make it meet
For the sowing of the wheat.

I would blight your team with blain,
I would rust your ploughs with rain,
In your furrows, deep and brown,
I would scatter thistle-down.

I would put twelve milking cows
On your pastures green to browse ;
I would set twelve tubs of cream
On your dairy's oaken beam.

Blasted by a curse of mine,
All your cows should ail and pine ;
From your fields I'd skim the dew—
Steal the cream away from you.

Under your grey apple trees
I would hive the honey bees ;
Store away in each gold dome
Lush, delicious honey-comb.

From the boughs of rose and grey
I would charm the bees away,
Bitter bread might be your share
On the days of Easter fare.

I would crown your head with gold,
Robe you fine in silken fold,
Win for you a magic wand
From Danaan fairy-land.

I would break your golden crown,
I would rend your silken gown,
I would burn your magic wand
From Danaan fairy-land.

I would place you on a throne,
I would give you all to own,
All of me and all of mine :
I would make you half-divine.

I would leave you in sore want,
I would have you hunger-gaunt,
I would bring you to my feet
In subjection most complete.

I would lift you to the skies,
I would give you paradise ;
I would suffer hell's worst dole
For the saving of your soul.

Wounding coldness to reprove
I would wound you in my love.
Suppliant still at your heart's gate
I do worship in my hate.

The Rann of Norna

I AM Norna of the nut-brown tresses,
    My home is a hut in the heart of the wood,
Where a fairy footfall the green moss presses,
And high in the branches the grey doves brood;
O sweet comes the wind from the far-off nesses,
Where the sea is a silver and azure flood!

My father is come of Heremon's stock:
He is soft as flour, he is hard as rock.
His blood for his friend, his sword for his foe—
Ah, this pagan law! 'tis a thing of woe.
How shall we plead for pardon, we
Whose sins are the grains of the sands of the sea,
While the ineffaceable words are writ:
" The judgment ye give, ye are judged by it."

My mother is born of a bardic race,
Amergin looks through her mystic eyes,
Fergus, the Druid, had such a face,
Or Ollav Fodhla, the mighty and wise,
Lore and love in her heart abide.
She is cunning as Mave and kind as Bride.

The wood-doves feed from her milken hand,
She passed the were-wolf by without scathe,
That robbed the graves in Emania's land,
And scattered the bones in its track of death.
Her foster-mother beheld her wraith
Walking the meads on the first of May—
There is in Erin an ancient faith
That whoso is seen hath a long, long day,
If she shall be warm when I am cold,
Blessed be Christ an hundred-fold !

Outside the door of our wattled house
The bee-hives stand in a golden row,
And the hum of the bees is murmurous
From the rose-red dawn till the sun's last glow.
An hundred kine are milked in the dew,
An hundred maids do spin in our hall,
An hundred flocks on the mountain blue
Gather when that our shepherds call,
And an hundred Fenians guard us all.

I am Norna of the nut-brown tresses,
Cathair, my lover is a prince of Saul.
No red stag roams through the wildernesses
With statelier mien than he treads the hall.
His hair is yellow as a leaf in Autumn,
His eyes are bright as the stars in frost,
Virtue and prayer his mother taught him,
His father learned him to lead a host.
He is slow to anger, he is swift to pardon,
He is loth to meddle in contentious strife,
More kind his mouth is, more rich his guerdon
To him who saves than who takes a life.

He is fearless as Dathi in brawl or battle,
Single-handed he fought with a score
When Brian Mac Art stole Bard Ethell's cattle—
Brian Mac Art, he stole no more.

They say I am not for a warrior's wife,
That my heart is craven, my spirit weak.
That I shrink from the battle and dread the
    strife—
Verily 'tis a truth they speak,
For my heart doth sicken at the sight of blood,
And the man turned beast in his savage mood.
O Bards, that sing of the clans out-faring,
And laud the might of the steady stroke,
When brother smites brother with axe unsparing
As the hewer hacks at the senseless oak—
Ye hear but the wind in the banners singing,
Ye hear but the rush of the arrows winging,
Ye see but the glint of the shining steel—
Your brain cannot think, your heart cannot feel!

Columcille, in his passionate youth,
Lifted the sword between North and South.
Sinning he stood on the bloody heath,
The vultures darkened the morning light,
Like a wind went the sob of the hard-drawn
    breath,
There were ruddy faces gone ashen white,
The hero of the resistless blade
Looked on his work—and was afraid !
Long was his penance, long and sore,
Banished to lone Iona's shore.

Strike for the right, if strike you must.
But glory not in the pride of war;
The body your stroke hath scattered to dust,
You shall answer to God therefor.
See that your battle-cause be just!

Cathair knows that I am no coward,
The blood of Heremon never ran cold.
I climbed the hill when the thick snow showered
To find the lamb that forsook the fold.
Waist-high, I forded the roaring river,
To bring the priest to a dying man,
I tended old Maureen in the plague of fever
When she lay forsaken of her own clan.

I am Norna of the nut-brown tresses,
And I love my lover, the prince of Saul.
I would not part with his kind caresses
To hold all Erin in willing thrall.
One enemy in all Erin I have—
The girl who would wile him away from me;
Yet even her (for Christ's sake) I would save
From death and danger by land or sea.

The Days o' the Spring

THE days o' the Spring do lightly pass,
  Hey, for the Summer and the red roses!
With opening bud and freshening grass
The days o' the Spring do lightly pass
For every lad and every lass,
And every bird in the orchard closes.
The days o' the Spring do lightly pass,
Hey, for the Summer and the red roses!

The King's Mercy

JOIN together the fragments
　　Of the shattered glass ;
Gather the wan, crushed petals
Of a rose that was ;
Wake the dead from her sleeping
Under the grass !

Dim is the rainbow crystal
That glistened so,
Winter is white on the mountains,
The dark broods low.
Rose and maiden are dreaming,
Shrouded in snow.

" I will bind up that which was broken."
Sayeth the King.
" The rose shall have reddest budding
In a heavenly Spring.
I will wake the maid from her sleeping,
And the stars shall sing."

My King

I WORSHIP him the livelong day,
  He never turns to look my way,
And yet my whole heart's sunshine lies
Within his eyes of dusky grey.

Those eyes are dreaming evermore
Of one sweet woman they adore;
I veil my grief with cunning art,
But oh, my heart is very sore!

Soft pink and white that pales and glows,
Her face is a delicious rose!
Her eyes where heaven's azure sleeps
Are starlit deeps of still repose.

The rowan berries blooming south
Are not so red as her red mouth,
Nor dewier they by woodland ways
In Autumn days of dust and drouth.

O fair is she, I know of none
More beautiful to look upon;
But whom my darling loves 'twere meet
That she be sweet as summer dawn.

Am I content? Hath jealousy
No sting wherewith to torture me?
Doth my weak soul obey in full
Christ's golden rule of charity?

Am I content? Should sun forsake
The wheat in June? Should Winter wake?
My nightingales have scarcely sung,
My heart is over-young to break!

O Fool! O Heart! O storm of pain
That beateth down my whitening grain!
O harvest-fields left desolate
To winds of hate and blasting rain!

Messages

GOD loosed His shining flock at even,
   And every little, gold bird came winging
Into the dim, grey heaven,
Sailing and singing.
Swift and eager in luminous flight
Through the breathing dark of the Summer night.
Ah, little birds,
With gold wings palpitating over the blue,
Whither go you,
Journeying by airy hill and hollow?
I fain would follow
Through the ways of heaven.
I, the man bereaven,
In whose heart is a wound as of a thousand
   swords.

On your heavenly road
You are so high, so high,
Can you see my sweetheart's face
By the crystal lattices,
When the gates of the House of God
You go faring by?
Her hair is a mist of light,
Her eyes are the eyes of a dove,
Her vesture is maiden-white,
She is my beautiful love!

I know you will find her, for sure,
Walking by Mary's side.
My lady, lily-pure!
My saint, all sanctified!

Tell her I bring a daffodil in March
To her grave under the larch;
A lily in Summer's prime,
A golden leaf in the harvest-time,
And red, red berries in the rime,
When desolate and chill,
The winds moan on the purple hill.

Tell her no maiden's face doth pleasure me
Save in its dear resembling of hers,
For any maiden's voice on land or sea
My sad heart never stirs.
No rose may blossom on *her* dead, young cheek,
Out from *her* grave no voice shall ever speak.
O birds of God!
Tell her I am with nor hope or succour
Since the day He took her
Into His rest.
Yea, the wolf of pain hath gnawed
To the very quivering core of the living heart
      in my breast!

Hie away!
Blue i' the east is the dawn o' the day.
And the eagle of the Sun
Would reign alone.
Out of his road!
Little star-birds, fly home to God!

57

A Philosopher

THE corn-crake crooned at night,
The fox-glove had blown,
The hawthorn was white,
The first meadow was mown.

There were roses in the sun,
There were roses in the shade,
But the lily stood alone,
Like a proud, matchless maid.

Along the garden walk
Were flecks of gold and grey;
I heard the rooks talk
In a tree far away.

I had smiled last year
For sake of these things,
For sun and wine-sweet air,
And fluttering of wings.

But now—could I find
Delight in merry June,
While she was lying blind
In sleep that came too soon ?

.   .   .   .   .

With outstretched, brown palms,
A beggar from the road,
Came asking for an alms,
For love of the dear God.

Withered he was, and old,
But under the white hair
His brow was broad and bold,
And honest as God's air.

Face, an ancient ruin,
And eyes, the crevices
That let heaven's blue in.
No hind was here, I wis.

Meat and white bread
Were pleasant to his mouth,
Milk was sweet as mead,
In a hot day's drouth.

" The heavens be your bed !—"
" God mark you to grace !—"
Another man had said
In this beggar's place.

But listen to his prayer,
Weigh the wisdom of it!
This philosopher
Did disdain to covet.

For my poor largesse,
Spake he in reward:
"A *taste* of happiness,
May ye get from the Lord!"

Well might I be content,
The Summer world was fair.
His way the old man went,
The sun on his white hair.

A March Song

DEAD is the dark Winter
   (O the primrose on the hill!)
March bloweth his fanfare
I' the horn o' the daffodil.

Rain water in the dykes
Is clear as amber glass ;
It feedeth the tall spikes
Of the high, green grass.

Earthward dancing sunbeams
Wave their wizard wands,
Flaggers into green flames
Flicker by the ponds.

O but March is kind!
At every road's edge
Sways on the warm wind
A budding thorn hedge.

And the crows have built their nest
I' the highest bough of the larch.
When the wind is from the west
Mild and kind is March !

In the Dargle

BY leaning fern and mossy stone
  The river singeth all alone
A musical, sweet monotone.

Within its lucent canopies
The sunbeam broodeth dreamy-wise,
Like to a smile in girlhood's eyes.

Athwart the amber and the snow
Of quiet pools 'twixt flow and flow,
The quiet birds flit to and fro.

You cannot hear if that they sing,
For the wild waters, murmuring,
Weep into silence everything.

Weep into silence : I have said.
The earthly voice being quieted,
I hear the voices of the dead.

They lie in happy graves afar,
Where no cliff climbeth high to bar
The shining of the evening star.

There stand the mountains, misty blue,
The soft, south heaven leaning to,
That holds the cisterns of the dew.

And when that dew doth thither sweep
To weep for them who cannot weep,
Methinks the dreamers smile in sleep.

Then, ere the smile hath wholly died
Upon their white brows, sanctified;
The dawn stands rosy as a bride,

And every bird doth wake for day.
(Whether the bough be green or grey,
The little birds do sing alway.)

O sweet amid the leafy falls
That tapestry their magic halls,
They pipe their golden madrigals!

O sweet, if that the dead may hear
This honeyed speaking, pure and clear,
In every day, in every year!

God calleth keeners for His own,
The dew shall weep when I am stone—
Shall rain its pity softly down.

And when the pain hath taken root
Within a heart, to strike it mute,
The bird shall murmur as a lute.

PRINTED BY R. FOLKARD AND SON,
22, DEVONSHIRE STREET, QUEEN SQUARE, BLOOMSBURY,
LONDON, W.C.